S0-BOB-510

OODLES OF DOODLES!

To Kate, Lexie and Lyric—
forever my family in laughter and love!
—A. K.

For Manie —C. J.

SIMON SPOTLIGHT
An imprint of Simon & Schuster Children's Publishing Division
1230 Avenue of the Americas, New York, New York 10020
This Simon Spotlight edition September 2022

Manufactured in the United States of America 0822 LAK
2 4 6 8 10 9 7 5 3 1
Library of Congress Cataloging-in-Publication Data
Names: Kontis, Alethea, author. | Jacques, Christophe, illustrator.
Title: Oodles of doodles! / by Alethea Kontis ; illustrated by Christophe Jacques.
Description: Simon Spotlight edition. | New York : Simon Spotlight, 2022. | Series: Ready-to-read.
Level 1 | Audience: Ages 4–6. | Audience: Grades K–1. | Summary: A poodle demonstrates his
ability to doodle oodles and oodles of noodles.
Identifiers: LCCN 2022009861 (print) | LCCN 2022009862 (ebook) | ISBN 9781665903806 (hc) |
ISBN 9781665903790 (pbk) | ISBN 9781665903813 (ebook)
Subjects: CYAC: Doodles—Fiction. | Poodles—Fiction. | Dogs—Fiction. | LCGFT: Animal fiction. |
Picture books.
Classification: LCC PZ7.K835518 Oo 2022 (print) | LCC PZ7.K835518 (ebook) | DDC [E]—dc23
LC record available at https://lccn.loc.gov/2022009861
LC ebook record available at https://lccn.loc.gov/2022009862

OODLES OF DOODLES!

written by **ALETHEA KONTIS**
illustrated by **CHRISTOPHE JACQUES**

Ready-to-Read

Simon Spotlight
New York London Toronto Sydney New Delhi

Hello!

Do you doodle?

I do doodle!

Do you doodle?

I do doodle!

Does your poodle doodle?

My poodle doodles
OODLES!

Could you doodle noodles?

I COULD doodle noodles!

Could your poodle
doodle noodles?

My poodle can doodle
OODLES of noodles!

I would love to have that doodle!

This doodle?

Or the poodle doodle?

The doodle two!

Let me noodle.
Hmm . . . can you
doodle a poodle?

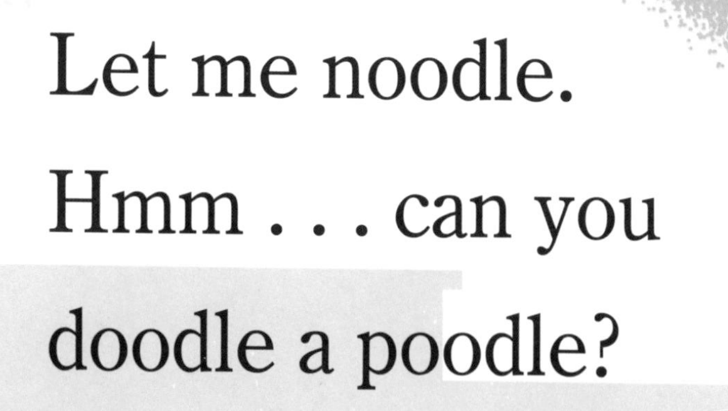

A poodle doodle?

For two doodles of noodles,
one by me,
one by my poodle!

Must I make this poodle doodle?

Oh, do.

Make him doodle!

Should he doodle noodles?

He SHOULD doodle noodles!

What if the poodle
in my doodle
doodles more poodles?

Yes!

Think of the doodles
we could doodle
with a caboodle
of doodling poodles!

Here is my poodle doodle for your two doodles of noodles.

Here are the doodles
of noodles,
by me and my poodle.

Thanks oodles!

Thank YOU oodles!

TOODLE-OO!

TOODLE-TOO!